Firefly

and
the Quest of
the Black Squirrel

J. H. Sweet

Illustrated by Tara Larsen Chang

SOURCEBOOKS
Jabberwocky
AN IMPRINT OF SOURCEBOOKS

D1364012

What follows is the original, unedited manuscript directly from the
author. It is her vision in its purest form.

Published by Sourcebooks Jabberwocky, an imprint of
Sourcebooks, Inc.
P.O. Box 4410, Naperville, Illinois 60567-4410
(630) 961-3900
Fax: (630) 961-2168
www.fairychronicles.com

Cataloging in Publication data is on file with the publisher.

ISBN-13: 978-1-4022-0875-1
ISBN-10: 1-4022-0875-8

Printed and bound in the United States of America.
LB 10 9 8 7 6 5 4 3 2 1

To Ed's parents,
for light and life

MEET THE

Firefly

NAME:
Lenox Hart

FAIRY NAME AND SPIRIT:
Firefly

WAND:
Single Piece of Straw

GIFT:
A great light within

MENTOR:
Mrs. Pelter,
Madam June Beetle

Thistle

NAME:
Grace Matthews

FAIRY NAME AND SPIRIT:
Thistle

WAND:
Porcupine Quill

GIFT:
Fierce and wild in
defending others

MENTOR:
Madam Robin

FAIRY TEAM

Marigold

NAME:
Beth Parish

FAIRY NAME AND SPIRIT:
Marigold

WAND:
Pussy Willow Branch

GIFT:
Can ward off nasty insects

MENTOR:
Aunt Evelyn,
Madam Monarch

Periwinkle

NAME:
Vinca Simpson

FAIRY NAME AND SPIRIT:
Perwinkle

WAND:
Elephant's Eyelash

GIFT:
Ability to channel energy from
the sun, resistant to heat

MENTOR:
Mrs. Welles,
Madam Rose

Inside you is the power to do anything

The Fairy Chronicles

Marigold and the Feather of Hope, the Journey Begins

∿

Dragonfly and the Web of Dreams

∿

Thistle and the Shell of Laughter

∿

Firefly and the Quest of the Black Squirrel

∿

Spiderwort and the Princess of Haiku

∿

Periwinkle and the Cave of Courage

Come visit us at fairychronicles.com

$\mathscr{C}$ontents

Chapter One: Spring Break **1**

Chapter Two: Camping **11**

Chapter Three: New Faces **27**
    at Fairy Circle

Chapter Four: The Black Squirrel **48**

Chapter Five: The Dwarf and the Squit **60**

Chapter Six: The Black Stag **77**

Chapter Seven: Blue Moon Clover **91**

Chapter Eight: The Shadow of Death **97**
    and the Light of Life

Fairy Fun **106**

Fairy Facts **108**

Chapter One

Spring Break

This was the most fun Lenox Hart ever had on spring break. She was camping for a whole week with her friends—Grace Matthews, Beth Parish, and Vinca Simpson. Beth's Aunt Evelyn was chaperoning and had reserved a campsite at a large, woodsy state park about thirty miles from the girls' homes.

Lenox was in home-school with her mother as the teacher. But every year, Mrs. Hart observed the same holiday schedule as the public schools, so Lenox got to spend a lot of time doing activities with her friends like sleepovers and camping trips.

Even though her brother had already left home for college, and there were no other children at her house during school, Lenox had a lot of friends. Her mother arranged crossover teaching with twelve other families who did home-schooling. Twice a week, Lenox traveled to other home-schools for group specialty subjects like sports, drama, music, art, and foreign language. Although she was only nine years old, Lenox was already learning both French and Spanish.

The parents of the home-schoolers also arranged field trips, usually twice a month, to places like museums and colleges, and to a variety of events such as county fairs and state cultural celebrations. Last week, they had taken a trip to a dairy farm to see milk being processed. Next month, they would all be going to see a play at a local college. So even though she didn't attend public school, Lenox had plenty of friends.

But she was especially close to Grace, Beth, and Vinca because she had something very special in common with them. In addition to being regular nine-year-olds, the girls were also fairies.

This was a very big secret to the girls' classmates and to most of the grown-ups they knew, including their parents. Fairy activities needed to be kept secret because fairies had an important job that sometimes included danger, and it would be hard for parents to understand why their daughters had to be away from home sometimes conducting risky fairy business.

Fairies were tasked with the important job of protecting nature and fixing serious problems, mainly problems caused by other magical creatures. It was a tremendous responsibility to be a fairy. Fairy powers could not be used for trivial matters or to solve personal problems. In fact, younger fairies were not supposed to perform magic at all without approval from an older fairy or mentor.

There were many different types of fairy spirits including birds, small animals, flowers, reptiles, berries, tiny sea creatures, herbs, tree blossoms, insects, and such like. Grace was a thistle fairy. Beth had the fairy spirit of a marigold. And Vinca's spirit was that of a periwinkle.

Lenox had been given a firefly fairy spirit. She held a light inside her greater than any other fairy, and was a source of brightness and inspiration to all who knew her. When Lenox was born, her mother noticed that even though her little girl was pale, she had a kind of shine and glow that was very unique and special. Because of this, Mrs. Hart had named her daughter after her set of beautiful Lenox china dishes.

Lenox had straight auburn hair and watery, hazel gray eyes that could change

colors with the light or her mood. Occasionally, her eyes looked very blue. Other times, they seemed to be silver. And sometimes, they were a greenish brown. It depended on the clothes she was wearing, what she was thinking, and the way the light was at any given moment.

In fairy form, Lenox had sparkling gold wings and wore a dress of glowing, golden brown silk. Her dress came to just above her knees; and she wore soft, fawn tan colored slippers to complete her fairy apparel. On her belt, she carried a little pouch of pixie dust, the fairy handbook, and her wand.

Lenox's wand was a single piece of bright, gleaming, golden straw. Fairy wands could be made from almost any object and were enchanted to help fairies perform magic. At first, Lenox had envied some of the fancier wands of other fairies. But as she had gotten older, she was more than content with her straw wand. They were a perfect team. Her wand contained a warmth and light of its own. When she held the straw in her hand, it connected with the light inside her and made her stronger.

Lenox's mentor was her neighbor, Mrs. Pelter, a June beetle fairy. Mrs. Pelter had lived next door to the Harts since before Lenox was born. She was known as Madam June Beetle to the younger fairies and was also supervising the girls' camping trip.

Beth's Aunt Evelyn was a monarch butterfly fairy and acted as Beth's mentor.

Most fairy mentors were older fairies, but Grace's mentor was a wise old robin. Madam Robin had been bewitched and could actually speak. But she was not present on the camping trip because it was springtime, and she was very busy visiting with other birds and building a nest.

In addition to camping, the girls had something else special to look forward to. They would all be attending a Fairy Circle the next day. Fairy Circles were gatherings of fairies held several times a year whenever there was a problem to be solved or if there was need for a fairy celebration.

This was the first time Vinca had ever been camping, and she was very excited about it. Vinca lived with a foster family. Her parents had passed away when she was five, and she had lived with three foster families so far. She currently lived with the Martinez family, and they were taking steps to legally adopt her. By the end of the summer, the paperwork would be complete, and Vinca would have a whole family again, this time for the rest of her life. She loved her new parents very much and got along well with her new ten-year-old sister, Megan.

Vinca's mentor was a yellow rose fairy named Mrs. Welles who was a social worker in the foster care system. Madam Rose was not going camping with the girls, but she would be at the Fairy Circle tomorrow.

Chapter Two

$\mathscr{C}$amping

Nearing dusk—in the large campsite, well away from the road and other campers—Firefly, Marigold, Thistle, Periwinkle, Madam Monarch, and Madam June Beetle all changed into fairy form. Standard fairy form was six inches high. They had arrived at the state park mid-morning to set up tents and unpack their gear. The tents shielded the fairies from other campers and the park rangers who passed by every so often.

Of course, if anyone happened to see them, the fairies would only look like a monarch butterfly, a June beetle, a firefly, and three tiny flowers. To non-magical people, fairies were only visible as their fairy spirits.

However, the fairies still had to be careful about being seen. Since this was the middle of March, it was not the right time of year for June beetles, which were usually seen May through July. And monarch butterflies mainly only migrated through this region of the country in February and October, so observant people might notice that it was the wrong time of year for these insects. Since it was early springtime, flowers were not that unusual. They could bloom anytime, spring through fall, and it would take a true flower expert to know which ones were out of season.

Each of the fairies had been given a special gift relating to her fairy spirit. Firefly's gift was her light. It lit dark places and helped to guide her. And she was seldom misled by bad spirits because her light could warn her of danger. The light was located somewhere around her stomach area and was actually very small, only about the size of a grain of sand. But it was extremely powerful. Firefly had never been afraid of the dark and was able to glow brightly enough to light great expanses of darkness if necessary.

Thistle had short, spiky blond hair and large gray eyes. In fairy form, she had tall, pointed, cloudy gray wings and a dress made of prickly, pale purple thistle petals. Her wand was a porcupine quill, and her special fairy gift was the ability to fiercely defend against attackers, just as a prickly wildflower could.

As a fairy, Marigold had pale gold wings and wore a crinkly, yellow and gold, marigold petal dress with a crown of tiny flowers to match.

She had curly brown hair, and her wand was an enchanted pussy willow branch. Marigold was gifted with the ability to ward off unfriendly insects. This was because marigold flowers had that quality in nature.

Periwinkle had long, straight dark hair. Her tiny pink wings were very feathery; and her dress was made of bright, rosy pink flower petals. She also wore a periwinkle flower on a hairclip by her left ear. Her wand was an elephant's eyelash.

The special gift of pink periwinkle flowers was their tolerance to the sun. In fact, the periwinkle flower was the most sun tolerant of any flower. As her unique fairy gift, Periwinkle was given the ability to channel energy from the sun and withstand intense heat. She loved the sunshine and spent as much time outdoors as possible. It gave her strength.

Periwinkle was of Native American ancestry. Her mother had been a Cherokee

Periwinkle

Indian. Because of her heritage, Periwinkle also had a spirit guide. He took the form of a small snail and traveled on her shoulder. However, Periwinkle was the only one who could see her tiny companion and hear his words of guidance.

Endurance and strength were Madam Monarch's special fairy gifts. This was similar to monarch butterflies in nature. They had enough stamina to migrate all the way from Canada to Mexico and back each year. Madam Monarch's wand was a single, sparkling dandelion seed.

Madam June Beetle's special fairy gift was also strength. She was a very hearty fairy with a tough outer shell, just like a June beetle. One time, an unfriendly locust had attacked her. He bounced right off of her and sailed about fifteen feet before landing. Madam June Beetle carried an enchanted red poppy flower for her wand.

As the sun went to sleep, the fairies gathered around one side of the concrete fire pit. Madam June Beetle lit a single charcoal briquette with her wand, and it glowed a brilliant orange red. The single piece of charcoal warmed the tiny fairies and was plenty hot enough to roast marshmallows, or rather, one marshmallow. A single marshmallow was enough for all of the fairies to share. They roasted chunks of it on pieces of wire.

Wood fires were not allowed in the park because of last summer's drought and concerns about forest fire danger. But even in years with plenty of rain, visitors to the park were not permitted to gather dried twigs, leaves, or wood to make fires because everyone had to follow the park's motto, *"Take only photographs."* The state park had rules about collecting things.

Beth had recently started collecting meteorites; and Lenox owned an extensive crystal, mineral, and fossil collection that she had been adding to for many years. But if they found any of these things in the state park, they could not take them home with them. Everything in the park had to be left for others to enjoy in the future.

The girls could not collect feathers, acorns, or leaves as they might in other wild places. Sometimes it was hard to leave a beautiful pinecone or brilliant autumn leaf behind, but the fairies knew the rules had a purpose. Generations from now, people would still be able to enjoy the park just as they did today.

While they sat around the fire, Vinca told her friends, "I think my mother might have known about my fairy spirit because the word vinca means exactly the same thing as periwinkle. It also means friendship."

As they roasted the marshmallow bits, Lenox told the others about her last visit with another friend named Jennifer Sommerset, a dragonfly fairy. "I had a sleepover at Jennifer's house last Saturday. I helped her and her grandmother take a load of glass and newspaper to the recycle center."

All fairies were invested in recycling, conservation, and preserving the environment, but Jennifer took her job more seriously than any other fairy. Anyone visiting her house was almost guaranteed to hear about her latest recycling efforts, or be involved in helping with some new project. Jennifer was not camping with her friends because she was taking a trip to Washington, D.C. with her mother and grandmother for spring break.

Grace, Beth, and Vinca all listened politely as Lenox went on with her story. "We also helped Mr. Wimple plant a row of white asparagus." (Mr. Wimple was the gnome who helped tend the Sommersets' garden.) None of the other girls knew about white asparagus so Lenox explained. "White asparagus grows entirely under ground. Sunlight never touches it. That's why it stays white and has a different taste than green asparagus. We planted the row

of asparagus crowns, just like the green asparagus. Then we mounded dirt up about a foot high all along the top of the new row.

"Mr. Wimple showed us the tool used to harvest white asparagus. It's long and forked on the end. When the tip of the asparagus reaches the top of the mound, it starts to turn purple. Before it grows taller, you push the tool into the mound and cut the stalk under ground. The sunlight never has a chance to turn the stalk green." Lenox finished the asparagus story with, "We're all invited to help cut white asparagus when it is ready to harvest."

Garden gnomes loved to share information and teach gardening secrets. And gnomes especially loved to work in the gardens of homes that had fairies because fairies could see and talk to them. Gnomes had to magically disguise themselves as ordinary objects around regular people. In fact, Jennifer's parents often saw Mr. Wimple, but thought he was a soccer ball, a butternut squash, or a fallen tree branch.

"Jennifer's mother promised to take lots of pictures on their trip," Lenox added. "They are going to see the Washington Monument, the Lincoln Memorial, and the Smithsonian Institution. Jennifer made me promise to keep journal notes about our camping trip and Fairy Circle, especially since there will be new fairies at our meeting."

Lenox laughed as she told her friends the final bit of information about her sleepover. "When I was there, I heard Jennifer's dad telling her mom that while all of the ladies were out of the house, he was going to do manly things like hammer on wood in his workshop, watch a lot of sports on television, and eat lots of junk food."

Lenox's mother was visiting her sister while Lenox was camping. Grace's mother was busy fixing up a nursery for Emily, Grace's baby sister, due to arrive in one month. And Beth's parents never needed an excuse to hand Beth over to her aunt for a week. Beth was quite the bundle of energy, and it was sometimes nice for her parents to have a break from her. Beth didn't mind this. She loved spending time with Aunt Evelyn.

Grace was looking forward to telling everyone at Fairy Circle that her little sister was going to have a fairy spirit too. Emily was going to be a buttercup fairy. So far, only her camping trip friends and Madam Robin knew about Buttercup.

While the girls were talking about the animals they had seen on the hiking trail that afternoon, a large hawk delivered a nut message to Madam June Beetle. Nut messages were hollowed-out nuts used for fairy communication. Notes and letters were hidden inside acorns, walnuts, hazel-

nuts, pecans, and such like. Then birds and animals delivered them for the fairies. The note was from Madam Toad, the leader of fairies for the Southwest region.

After reading the message carefully, Madam June Beetle told them, "I'm afraid we will have to cut our camping trip short, girls. After Fairy Circle tomorrow, we will all be going on a very important mission that will take most of the week. Madam Toad didn't give any other details. We'll find out more at the meeting."

After cleaning up around the campsite and dousing the charcoal with water and dirt, they all went to bed, wondering what new adventure awaited them tomorrow.

Chapter Three

New Faces

at Fairy Circle

The girls packed up their camp at first light after a quick breakfast of cereal and apples. They carefully checked the campsite for forgotten items and trash, so the area was completely clean when Madam June Beetle did her inspection. "Good job, girls," she praised.

"*'Leave only footprints,'*" said Firefly, reciting one of their fairy mottos, also used by many parks.

Then the fairies all buckled up in Aunt Evelyn's lime green station wagon and were on their way. After driving for almost an

hour, they turned onto a small country road on the outskirts of a large forest.

Over half of the forest was designated as a nature preserve. And because it contained some endangered species of plants and animals, there were restrictions as to who could visit. No camping, hiking, or hunting was allowed. Geologists, botanists, and zoologists sometimes did research in the forest; but otherwise, it was pretty much deserted, except for the animals, insects, birds, and magical creatures that lived there. The technical name for the area was the Howell Nature Preserve, named after the family who first donated the land to the government. But so few people visited these woods that many people referred to it as the Forgotten Forest.

Aunt Evelyn parked in a small pullout by an area of public land just next to the preserve. With six small *pops*, the fairies changed into fairy form and flew into the Forgotten Forest to find the place Madam Toad had chosen for their gathering.

Madam Toad always chose the sites for Fairy Circles very carefully. They usually met under trees that had a special significance to the purpose of their meeting. This time, the fairies were meeting under a silver fir that was standing next to a walnut tree. Many of the forest trees were still bare from winter, but the silver fir was an evergreen. It was healthy and full, and very fragrant. The fairies smiled at each other as they breathed in the piney smell. The walnut tree had buds on it where the leaves were ready to spring out as the weather grew warmer.

As they approached the tree, Madam June Beetle told the girls, "I'm not sure why we are meeting under a silver fir. Silver fir trees are symbolic of success in finding something that is sought. Maybe we will be taking a journey to find something."

And Firefly added, "But walnut trees stand for healing, so maybe we will be helping to fix something that needs to be healed."

Madam Toad always allowed the fairies to visit for awhile before beginning their group discussions. Today, they would be welcoming several new fairies to Fairy Circle. Many of the fairies had come early to allow plenty of time to get to know their new friends.

As Firefly's group arrived, Rachel, the morning glory fairy, came running to greet them. She was dragging a tiny, dustywing skipper butterfly fairy by the hand. Morning Glory was nine and was very excited to have her little sister attend Fairy Circle for the first time.

Morning Glory was very beautiful in a dress of vivid blue with soft green morning glory vines creeping in circles around her hips and waist, and crawling up to curl over her shoulders. The dark, sky-blue flowers dangling from the vines were streaked with white in the centers and were very bright. She also had a small morning glory vine circling the crown of her head and tying her hair into a ponytail. The blue flowers were a lovely contrast to her shining, reddish-brown hair. Her wand was a polished splinter of mahogany, and she carried it in her belt.

Morning Glory arrived in front of them a little breathless. "This is Skipper, I mean Kayla, my sister. She's seven. She just found out about her fairy spirit two weeks ago. I've been teaching her to fly and how to use her handbook."

Since Morning Glory was out of breath to start with, and hadn't taken a breath while introducing Skipper, she had to pause for a gulp of air before trying to introduce the newly arrived fairies to her sister. Firefly smiled and quickly made the introductions for her so Morning Glory could catch her breath.

Skipper giggled and flushed a little, clutching her yellow tulip wand in one hand while shaking their hands with the other. Skipper's dress was a dark, charcoal gray; and her wings were black with dusty, purplish-gray streaks. She had a yellow belt and slippers to match her wand, and her light brown hair was pulled back to one side with a bright yellow tulip barrette. Skipper had barely finished shaking hands with everyone when Morning Glory whisked her off to meet other fairies.

The next fairy the girls met was Madam Chameleon. She was not new. In fact, she had been in the region for a long time but had been unable to attend their last few

Fairy Circles, so the girls had not had a chance to meet her until today.

Firefly, Thistle, Marigold, and Periwinkle actually weren't able to see Madam Chameleon at first because she was the exact pale gray color all over as the smooth stone she was sitting on. When she spoke to them, they all jumped. As she got up and came to stand next to the trunk of the silver fir, she turned the exact grayish-brown color of the tree trunk. It was a little unnerving not to be able to see her clearly.

When she was in-between changes, Madam Chameleon was a silvery greenish-blue color. The fairies wished she would stay that color so they could see her more easily; but apparently, Madam Chameleon didn't feel the need to control her color changes. However, when they watched closely, the girls were able to see Madam Chameleon's wand hovering about. It was a tiny sprig of mistletoe with a yellowish-green stem and leaves, and pearly white berries. So the young fairies tried to keep an eye out for the wand to pinpoint Madam Chameleon's location.

A new snapdragon fairy was not quite as comfortable as Skipper in meeting strange fairies. She huddled close to her mentor, a swallowtail butterfly fairy. Madam Swallowtail had her arm protectively around Snapdragon's shoulders as they approached Firefly and the others. "This is Bettina," said Madam Swallowtail.

Snapdragon was eight years old. She was wearing a fluffy, orange and yellow dress made of furled snapdragon petals. She looked very nervous and shy as she whispered, "Hello."

The whole fairy experience had been overwhelming so far for Snapdragon. She was holding her wand with two fingers, out away from her, as though afraid it might bite her. The apparently frightening wand was a black boar bristle, curled into a long spiral like a corkscrew. Madam Swallowtail's white clover blossom wand was tucked into the belt of her dress. As she led Snapdragon away, the fairy mentor took the boar bristle wand and tucked it into her belt next to the clover blossom for safekeeping.

Firefly, Marigold, Thistle, and Periwinkle were very interested in the many kinds of wands at Fairy Circle. Over the last year or so, they hadn't even seen all of the different wands of fairies they already knew. Now, they were getting to see an even greater variety. The girls stood in little groups to compare.

Spiderwort had a red cardinal feather for her wand. And Rosemary carried a wand made of rust-colored orangutan hairs. She showed it to them proudly, stating, "It has nine orangutan hairs, triple braided." Tulip carried a long crystal shard for her wand, and Lily's was a bluebird

feather. Firefly still liked her gleaming straw wand best, but next to hers, she thought Periwinkle's elephant's eyelash was the most interesting.

The girls approached their friend, Primrose, next to meet the new fairy she was standing with. The new fairy was Hollyhock, her cousin. Hollyhock was unique among fairies because she was the only fairy who was deaf. But she could read lips very well, and understood nearly everything that was said to her as long as she was standing close enough to see other people's mouths clearly.

Madam Swallowtail was mentor for Primrose and Hollyhock. Both Primrose and Madam Swallowtail knew sign language and were able to interpret for Hollyhock so she could easily understand the other fairies' conversations.

Firefly and Madam June Beetle helped to set up refreshments for everyone. While they visited, the fairies enjoyed powdered sugar puff pastries, homemade fudge, peanut butter and marshmallow créme sandwiches, raspberries, and lemon jellybeans. And they drank cool, sweet nectar and pomegranate juice from real honeysuckle blossoms.

There was also another new fairy, only six years old, whose spirit was that of a pumpkinwing butterfly. She had creamy orange wings with soft brown accents. But the other fairies didn't get to meet Pumpkinwing right away because she was sleeping, curled up in a little ball next to Madam Toad who was her mentor. Evidently she was tired, and it was naptime. Her mouth was open slightly as she slept. She looked very angelic with her short brown hair lying in soft curls on her

forehead, a peaceful expression on her face, and very rosy pink cheeks.

Madam Toad did not ordinarily mentor young fairies. She was usually too busy being the fairy leader, but she was making an exception because Pumpkinwing was her great-granddaughter.

Quite a few mentors were able to attend Fairy Circle this time, more than usual. Madam Rose was visiting with Madam Finch and Madam Chameleon. Thinking about the future, Firefly said to her friends, "It's funny to think that someday we'll be mentors. Can you imagine someone calling me, Madam Firefly?"

Thistle laughed, snorting with merriment, as she said, "And me, Madam Thistle." Still laughing, she bowed to Marigold and added, "I am pleased to meet you, Madam Marigold."

The girls were still laughing when Madam Toad called the meeting to order.

When she spoke, it was clear why Madam Toad was their leader. Her voice was very strong, precise, and loud, commanding everyone's attention. "Welcome! Welcome, everyone! We have many newcomers today. We are happy to have Skipper, Snapdragon, Hollyhock, and Pumpkinwing join us."

Pumpkinwing woke up at the sound of her name, yawned, stretched, and looked around at the rest of the fairies with wide, wondering blue eyes. Then she giggled a little and set to work on a plate of refreshments that Madam Toad had put aside for her. With lemon jellybeans in one hand and raspberries in the other, she continued to watch the rest of the fairies. She giggled again when Madam Chameleon took a seat on a mushroom and changed to a light, speckled brown color.

Skipper was evidently so excited to be at her first Fairy Circle that her wings started moving on their own, and she rose about a foot into the air. Morning Glory flew up to her sister and pulled her back down. Clearly, they would need more flying practice so Skipper could learn to control her wings.

Snapdragon sat close to Madam Swallowtail, who still had her arm around her.

And Hollyhock was watching Primrose, who was carefully interpreting Madam Toad's words in sign language. Madam Toad mentioned this to the group. "Either Primrose or Madam Swallowtail will be our sign language interpreter for our meetings. They will also begin teaching us American Sign Language. We will first learn the alphabet so we can fingerspell. Then we will progress to words and sentences. But our time together is limited. I encourage each of you to take sign language classes if you can. There are some excellent classes offered through continuing education at the local high schools and at the community college." The other fairies all nodded and were looking forward to learning sign language.

Madam Toad went on. "I hate to put a damper on our festivities, but we have a very serious problem to discuss today. However, before I introduce our guest speaker, I have something else important, and very sad, to tell you." She paused for a moment, looking down at the ground.

When the fairy leader started speaking again, her voice was extremely serious and stern. The entire group of fairies watched her closely. Though Madam Toad's voice was low and quiet, the tone of it was terrible. "Magnolia will no longer be joining us. She misused fairy magic in January. When she was given a second chance last month, she abused her power again. Her fairy spirit has been taken from her."

The other fairies were shocked, and looked around at one another in disbelief. They all knew Magnolia, whose name was

Constance, and it was hard to believe she would have done something to risk losing her fairy spirit.

The group remained silent as Madam Toad continued. "I cannot share the exact details of her actions, but I am reminding everyone of the responsibility that comes with being a fairy. You are never allowed to use fairy magic or fairy gifts in a trivial manner, or to abuse others. And younger fairies are never, *NEVER*, to use fairy magic unless supervised by a fairy mentor. I know your mentors have gone over this with you, but I am telling you again. You risk the wrath of Mother Nature and the wrath of me. You are *NEVER* to abuse fairy power! We have a specific purpose for being here, and we will stick to our jobs!"

No one said anything for several minutes. None of the girls could ever imagine someone willing to risk the wrath of Mother Nature. She was the guardian of fairies and other magical creatures, and the supervisor of all nature. Mother Nature was often in dangerous forms like flood, tidal wave, and blizzard. They could never count on her being in a safe form like frost, breeze, or sea mist.

Snapdragon had started crying. Madam Swallowtail gave the young fairy a drink of water, and with her arms around her, the fairy mentor rocked Snapdragon back and forth, trying to comfort her. Spiderwort was also crying. Magnolia had been a good friend.

Madam Toad realized that what she had told them was very upsetting. She waited a few moments longer before going on. When she began speaking again, her voice sounded kinder and less dreadful. "If you see Constance," the fairy leader said softly, "do not mention anything about fairies to her. Her memory has been cleared of all fairy activities and knowledge. She would not know what you are talking about, and it would confuse her or possibly frighten her."

Firefly, Marigold, Periwinkle, and Thistle all sat quietly, thinking how horrible it would be if their fairy spirits were taken from them, and how sad it was that Magnolia would never remember any of the wonderful things about being a fairy. Periwinkle's snail spirit guide, perched on her shoulder, sighed and shook his head sadly.

Next, Madam Toad cleared her throat and said, "Now, let me introduce our guest for today." As she said this, a small, solid-black squirrel stepped out from behind the trunk of the silver fir.

Chapter Four

The Black Squirrel

he black squirrel said something in low tones to Madam Toad. She responded with a small nod, and the squirrel stepped forward, preparing to speak.

Madam June Beetle was huddled close to Firefly, Thistle, Marigold, and Periwinkle, and she whispered to them. "He is a long way from home. Black squirrels are not usually seen this far South." The girls nodded in agreement. None of them had ever seen a black squirrel before.

The black squirrel looked nervous. When he spoke, his soft voice quavered a little at

the Black Squirrel

first. "First of all, I need to tell you that squirrels do not usually speak. I have been bewitched by Mother Nature to speak for one week only in order to communicate better with you. I have made a long journey to be here, from the far North. I live in a colony of black squirrels, and tragedy has befallen us. A terrible sickness has struck several black squirrel colonies in the far North, and it is spreading. The sickness causes death. None of the infected squirrels have died yet, but they will soon."

He paused for a few seconds while thinking of his next words. "Sometimes, widespread illness and death among animal species is normal," the squirrel told the fairies. "It is a means of nature taking care of overpopulation problems. For example, ten years ago, a plague-like disease spread through the prairie dogs of Southern Utah. Their numbers went from thousands down to about three hundred. But this was necessary. Three hundred prairie dogs were enough to repopulate the species; and now, they are not starving from overpopulation.

"This also happened in Montana with snowshoe hares about fifteen years ago. But we all know how fast rabbits multiply. They are fine and in vast numbers today.

"But what is happening to the black squirrels is not normal or natural. It is a curse." He paused again and took a deep shuddering breath before resuming his story. "A goblin named Anathema Bane created a *Perfect Curse*. *Perfect Curses* are very rare. In short, *Perfect Curses* are complete and irreversible. Anathema researched, studied, consulted dark witches, and drew on her own evil spirit to create and execute the curse. This dark spell will kill all black squirrels within one month."

The black squirrel stopped his story for a moment. When he started speaking

Anathema Bane

again, his voice shook. "But I haven't told you the worst part. The curse is a *Calendar-Chain-Curse*, set up to attack a new species each month. Next month, all white-tailed deer will die. In May, beavers, and the following month, earthworms. In July, snow geese, and so on. Eventually, it will reach humans. There is no stopping it." He sighed again and repeated, "It is a *Perfect Curse*."

But as the squirrel went on, his tone became lighter and more hopeful. "Mother Nature has told me that one cure can heal the sick squirrels. If blue moon clover is administered to every sick squirrel, we can stop the curse from spreading to other species. At this point, the sickness can only be spread to other black squirrels, so no other animals are in danger until April.

"Blue moon clover only grows in the Forgotten Forest. It can only be found by the Black Stag. And only a dwarf knows how to find the Black Stag. Mother Nature has told me how to find the dwarf. We must seek him out first. I need your help on this quest. We must obtain blue moon clover quickly. Some witches keep small quantities of dried blue moon clover, but we need a great amount, and it needs to be fresh to be potent enough to cure the sickness."

All of the fairies were very distressed by what the black squirrel had told them. Many were shaking, pale, and had terrified looks upon their faces. At last, Firefly could contain herself no longer. "But why?" she cried, struggling to hold back tears. "Why would Anathema do such a terrible thing?"

After a few moments of silence, Madam Toad answered her question. "Because she could." Again there was silence, then Madam Toad explained further. "As far as we know, all goblins are evil. And some creatures, blessed with knowledge and ability, use their powers to harm others. Not everyone can handle the responsibility that comes with power, and many do not choose their actions wisely. But there are consequences."

The black squirrel nodded and told them, "Mother Nature has taken care of Anathema Bane. She was in quicksand form when they met." The fairies all shuddered as he went on. "It was necessary. She would have been able to repeat the curse. It has been many ages since anyone has used a *Perfect Curse*. That I should see it in my lifetime." He shook his head sadly.

Her nerves finally totally frazzled, Spiderwort broke down and sobbed, shaking her head. "This is too much. I am not ready to be a fairy."

Several other fairies were crying too. Madam Toad took control of matters and firmly told them, "Everyone, stay calm. We will be able to find blue moon clover and stop the curse. Remember, fairies are fixers and problem solvers; and we have never failed on a mission.

"It will be a two-day journey each way," she added. "I have decided that Firefly will lead this mission, guided by her light. She will be accompanied by Periwinkle, Thistle, and Marigold. Madam June Beetle and Madam Monarch will supervise. The gifts of each of these fairies will combine to form a powerful team. There is guidance, strength, endurance, skill, intelligence, toughness, energy, and the ability to defend if necessary."

Next, Madam Toad addressed Periwinkle personally. "I am especially counting on you, Periwinkle, and your Native American skills. You should be able to keep the group from getting lost. Also, if you run out of food and need to eat any forest plants, you can steer everyone away from poison toadstools and toward edible mushrooms."

Periwinkle nodded, as her spirit guide whispered encouragingly in her ear. "We can handle this; everything will be fine."

Backpacks had already been readied for the fairies. Their provisions included pillows, blankets, water, peanut butter and marshmallow créme sandwiches, lemon jellybeans, and raspberries. And Madam June Beetle carried a water purifier, in case they ran out of water and needed to drink from streams, ponds, or lakes. She also had a separate bag full of sacks to hold the blue moon clover when they found it.

As they were preparing to leave, a badger lumbered up to the Fairy Circle and dropped off three pecans for the squirrel. The black squirrel explained,

"The brownies have arranged for animals to deliver food to me during our trip, so I won't have to take time to find any."

Brownies were boy fairies and were very good friends to animals and birds. In fact, they had a special partnership with them. Since brownies couldn't fly, birds and animals carried them when they needed to travel.

The black squirrel thanked the badger and ate quickly.

As the group departed on their mission, the other fairies wished them luck. And Madam Toad bid them farewell with her familiar parting words. "Flitter forth fairies and take care of business."

Chapter Five

The *D*warf and the *S*quit

The black squirrel knew exactly which route to take to find the dwarf, and Firefly's light assured them they were traveling in the right direction. Her light seldom allowed her to be misled, so all she had to do was trust and follow.

They only met one obstacle on the first part of the trip—a wide, fast moving river. The fairies could fly over, but the squirrel was not a very good swimmer. Firefly and Periwinkle scouted downriver and found a fairly shallow, narrow place with many stones to help the squirrel to cross. Then after they

crossed, Periwinkle led the group back upriver to pick up the trail.

As they traveled, Firefly looked up blue moon clover in her handbook and read the entry aloud to the others:

"*Blue Moon Clover: Blue moon clover grows only during the most rare type of blue moon, and can only be found by the Black Stag. It is a plant that does not die; instead, it waits to be found. Blue moon clover has magical healing properties that can cure many illnesses.*"

The fairies noticed that after the trip over the river, the black squirrel looked very tired and was out of breath. They slowed the pace a bit to give him a chance to rest.

Marigold flew close to his ear and talked to him. "We know several brownies and have worked with them on our missions before. Maybe we have some brownie friends in common."

The squirrel responded, nodding. "I carried Brownie Alan on a journey last month. He mentioned you several times on our trip."

Marigold didn't say anything to this, but she did blush a little. She had met Alan last summer and had kept in touch with him through nut messages. The black squirrel whispered quietly to her. "When our journey is finished, I can carry a message to him for you, if you like." Marigold smiled and nodded.

The slower pace allowed the squirrel to catch his breath and regain some of his strength. As they traveled, he told them, "Since our trip is under special circumstances, Mother Nature informed me that there will be a spring hailstorm tonight. If we are not able to stay at the dwarf's home, we will need to find shelter."

As she glowed brightly, leading the group through a dense, darker part of the forest, Firefly looked up dwarf in her handbook. The fairies and squirrel listened as she read the definition aloud:

> "*Dwarves: Dwarves are magical creatures, slightly larger than elves and slightly smaller than trolls, which means that they vary in height from three to four feet tall. They generally live in caves or old mines. Dwarves are skilled craftsmen and enjoy working with different types of metal and stone. It is unknown how far their magical abilities extend. Dwarf magic is very powerful and mysterious, primarily because dwarves are masters of keeping secrets. In fact, they specialize in secrets. They usually keep to themselves and only share*

their names with other dwarves. However, if a dwarf extends friendship to another creature, he will be a fierce and loyal ally for life. Dwarves tend to be somewhat greedy, seeking wealth and hoarding riches."

It was nearly dark by the time they reached the dwarf's home, which was an abandoned mine tucked into the side of a hill. The entrance was hard to see because the area was overgrown. Tangled tree limbs and vines partially shielded the front door. A closer look at the door revealed beautiful, intricately wrought ironwork hinges and locks, and a fancy brass doorknob. There was also a small, granite stone bench beside the door with scroll carvings across the seat and on the legs.

Firefly knocked on the door as loudly as she could with her small fist.

The dwarf opened the door almost at once. "Well, well, well…fairies and a black squirrel. This is quite a surprise."

Firefly introduced each fairy and the black squirrel to the dwarf. The dwarf said hello, but true to dwarf fashion, didn't give his name. Instead, he said, "You can call me, Dwarf." Smiling, he invited them inside.

In the entryway of his home, he lit several ornate metal and glass lanterns. He carried them into a widened area of the mine's entrance, placing them about the room for light. The dwarf obviously used this part of the mine as his living room. It was filled with wooden and stone chairs and tables of varying shapes and sizes.

The fairies and squirrel didn't have a chance to notice much of anything else around them because what looked like a furry, bright red ball bounced into the room. It was some kind of fluffy creature about the size of a soccer ball; and it made gulping, snorting noises as it bounced.

"This is my squit," said the dwarf. "His name is Firecracker."

Firecracker continued to bounce around the room—off walls, furniture, and even the ceiling. He was like a piece of popcorn that kept popping.

None of the fairies, or the black squirrel, had ever seen a squit before. The dwarf seemed to know this because he explained, "Squits are forest creatures, and they can't be seen by regular human beings. Their job in the woods is to spread mushroom spores and mosses around with their feet. See his fat little feet." The fairies barely caught a glimpse of feet as Firecracker flew past them. "Squits like living with dwarves. They can be any color."

As Firecracker whizzed by once again, the dwarf added, "He's catching air flies. Air flies are invisible to everyone except

the **Dwarf** & Firecracker, the **Squit**

squits." Firecracker paused briefly in his bouncing to belch loudly, as if in evidence of the large number of air flies he had consumed. The fairies laughed, and Firecracker resumed the popping and fly catching.

As Firefly and the black squirrel explained the purpose of their visit, the dwarf laid out a large, lavish supper for them. There were many kinds of nuts, berries, and other fruits. They also ate crackers and cheese and had lemonade to drink.

The dwarf waited until everyone had finished eating before addressing them. "I'm sorry, but I don't think I can help you."

No one said anything for a moment, but stared at the dwarf. Then Firefly said, "But Mother Nature sent us to ask for your help."

"Why didn't she come talk to me herself?" asked the dwarf.

"She is very busy," answered Firefly, a bit put out by the question.

"And very powerful," added Marigold.

The black squirrel chimed in squeakily, "And she can be very dangerous. Fortunately, she was in dust devil form when I met with her so I only got a bit of dust in my ears and nose. It could have been much worse. Believe me, you don't want to meet with her if you can help it." He coughed a little as he finished, looking even more tired, and now, a bit frazzled and desperate.

It had never occurred to any of the fairies or the black squirrel that the dwarf might not tell them how to find the Black Stag.

"Let me explain my position," the dwarf said. "I alone am entrusted with the secret of the location of the Black Stag. He is the last of his kind. Alone. He has been gifted with long life, speech, and the ability to find blue moon clover. But he is not invincible, or immortal. If someone sought to do him harm, he could not stop them."

"But we must find him," pleaded Firefly. "Do you not understand how many will die if we don't?"

"Your quest is very honorable, and I believe it is genuine. But what if the goblin has followed you to learn the location of the Black Stag to destroy him?" countered the dwarf.

The black squirrel answered earnestly. "She cannot follow, for she exists no longer. Mother Nature has ensured that Anathema Bane can never curse again."

The dwarf was silent for some minutes, studying the black squirrel keenly. "Can you prove that you met with Mother Nature?" he finally asked, looking intently into the black squirrel's eyes.

The squirrel thought for a few moments, then answered. "Yes, I can. There will be a hailstorm tonight at exactly 10:18 p.m. Mother Nature warned me that we would need to take cover. She usually doesn't give warnings, but since we were asked to make this difficult journey, she made an exception."

"Very well," said the dwarf. "At 10:19 p.m., I will tell you the location of the Black Stag."

The squirrel and the fairies were very relieved. Then the dwarf added, "I'm sorry I made you jump through hoops, but I have to be very careful. It is an important secret that I keep. You can all stay with me tonight to escape the storm, then leave first thing in the morning."

While they waited for the hailstorm, Marigold, Thistle, Periwinkle, Madam Monarch, and Madam June Beetle sat visiting with the dwarf as they watched Firecracker pop about catching more air flies.

Firefly went to talk to the black squirrel, sitting by himself in a quiet corner of the room. He looked very weak. Several acorns, delivered by a large tawny owl, lay beside him. Since the dwarf had provided plenty of nuts for supper, the squirrel was saving his acorns for breakfast.

"You've been infected with the sickness, haven't you?" Firefly asked.

"Yes," he answered quietly. "I don't have long to live, but I'm not worried about that. I must find blue moon clover to send back to the black squirrel colonies. Nothing else matters."

"Of course it matters," said Firefly. "You are important. All life is important. And you shouldn't worry so much right now. The fairies of this region have never failed in a mission. We will find the Black Stag and the clover tomorrow; I promise. Right now, you should rest." Firefly's assurance was so firm and her conviction so strong that the black squirrel was able to rest more easily.

At 10:18 p.m. the hailstorm began, and it was extremely loud and scary. The pounding hail was accompanied by thunder, making the storm sound like a weird

kind of music made by hammers and
drums, mixed up with wind and rain. Several hailstones rolled through a wide crack
under the dwarf's front door. The fairies
busied themselves with rolling the knee-
high hailstones back out again through
the same crack.

As promised, at 10:19 p.m., the dwarf,
gave Firefly and the black squirrel
instructions for how to find the Black
Stag. "You must head directly east when
you leave here. Pass through the forest,
always east, until you reach the purple
meadow. Cross through the purple
meadow to the white meadow. When you
cross the white meadow, you will come to
a third meadow—the Forgotten Meadow.
In the Forgotten Meadow, you will find
the Black Stag."

Next, the fairies made up beds with
their blankets and pillows in the same quiet
corner where the squirrel had chosen to

rest, while the dwarf shooed Firecracker into one of the empty mine shafts so his bouncing would not disturb them. Then they all drifted wearily off to sleep.

Chapter Six

The Black Stag

As they were leaving the next morning, the black squirrel presented the dwarf with a tiny golden acorn, about the size of a small pea, as a gift for his help. The dwarf thanked the black squirrel kindly and wished them all good luck.

Firefly led them east, towards the rising sun. As the group flew along, she exclaimed, "I remember what I wanted to do last night—look up blue moon in my handbook." When she found the entry, she said, "It's a long one." But the others were anxious to hear, so they listened carefully as she read to them:

"*Blue Moon:* 'Once in a blue moon' is a phrase used to describe something that does not occur very often, or something that is extremely rare. When referring to the moon itself, there are many definitions of blue moon. The most common type of blue moon refers to the second full moon occurring in one calendar month. This happens about once every two and a half years.

Blue moon can also mean the third full moon in a season with four. If any season (spring, summer, fall, or winter) has four full moons, the third full moon is called the blue moon.

The most rare type of blue moon occurs when the moon actually does turn blue. The reason for this lies in volcanic dust particles in the

fairies and squirrels, and these hornets were gaining on them, so the fairies turned to face them. Thistle, Marigold, and Madam June Beetle took the lead while Firefly, Periwinkle, and Madam Monarch hovered close to the black squirrel behind them.

One of the hornets rushed at Madam June Beetle, but she was so tough that he bounced right off her. Thistle lunged forward with her porcupine quill wand and managed to poke one of the advancing insects. The hornet buzzed angrily. There were about thirty hornets facing the fairies menacingly. Madam June Beetle pointed her poppy wand and sent orange sparks flying at the advancing insects, to warn them off. But there were too many of them.

Marigold felt afraid, but she also felt a surge of strength and power growing in her middle. It quickly extended out to her arms and legs, and seemed to be spilling right out of the top of her head. She held her hand up in front of her as though placing it flat on a wall. The force flowing out of her hand pushed back the cloud of hornets about a foot. Marigold was trying to be careful not to hurt any of the hornets. She simply wanted them to go away.

But the hornets didn't back down. If anything, they seemed to get angrier. They pushed hard against her force, trying to get near enough to sting the fairies and squirrel. Closer and closer they came.

"ENOUGH!" shouted Marigold. With this cry, she raised both hands against the hornets. The power that shot from her palms was strong enough to knock the hornets backwards nearly twenty feet. The swarm of insects landed in a dusty heap—stunned, squirming, buzzing, and trying to get up.

Marigold did not like what her power had done to the hornets, but she wasn't going to let any of her friends get stung.

The group quietly moved along, slowing their pace further because the black squirrel was growing weaker.

Suddenly, a gray fox appeared trotting beside them. The black squirrel spoke to him, and the fox nodded back. Relieved, the squirrel told the fairies, "The brownies have sent this fox to help me travel." The group paused for a moment while the fox sat down and allowed the squirrel to climb onto his back. Then the black squirrel rested while the strong fox carried him. The fairies were happy that he had help.

A little while later, Periwinkle steered the group away from a patch of poison ivy, and the rest of their journey through the woods was free from peril.

By lunchtime, they had reached the purple meadow. Lush clumps of purple

clover blossoms covered the ground. The group stopped briefly to rest and have lunch. Firefly looked up things in her handbook while they ate.

"Oh good, squit is in here," she said, and again she read aloud to them:

"Squits: Squits are fluffy, furry, magical creatures, invisible to regular people. When dry, they are about as large as basketballs. When wet, they are about the size of baseballs. Adults can be any color, but squitlings are usually light purple. Squits generally live with dwarves. They like to bounce around catching and eating air flies. In forested areas, their bouncing serves the purpose of spreading lichen, mosses, and mushroom spores. The plant bits are carried from place to place on the squits' fat feet."

Firefly paused for several seconds, reading a few lines ahead. "Oh my gosh!" she exclaimed. "Listen to this!"

"*Important Alternate Definition:* It is possible that squits do not exist. Some think they are a dwarf mind trick. Dwarf magic is largely mysterious and secret. No one has ever seen a squit without a dwarf nearby. And squits bounce around so fast that no one can ever catch them. Some believe that dwarves can create the vision of a squit. The squit then distracts visitors, drawing attention away from dwarf riches."

"Did anyone actually touch the squit?" Firefly asked.

They shook their heads, and Marigold said, "He was moving too fast."

And Thistle added, "I didn't see any of the dwarf's riches because I was watching the squit. Maybe it *was* a magical mind trick."

Firefly then asked the opinion of her mentor. Madam June Beetle sat thinking for a few moments before answering. "I want to believe they exist," she said simply.

The other fairies nodded in agreement. Madam Monarch smiled but didn't comment.

After lunch, the fairies, fox, and squirrel crossed the purple meadow and came to the white meadow. It too was filled with clover, but with white blossoms. The travelers noticed a great many spring bees buzzing about gathering pollen and nectar. Several of the insects flitted close to the fairies and greeted them with little tickly hello buzzes.

When they had crossed the white meadow, the group finally came to the Forgotten Meadow. It was filled with a kind of clover that had no blossoms. In the middle of the meadow, looking very majestic, stood the Black Stag. He was very large and solid black with huge, towering black antlers. His entire body glistened brilliantly in the afternoon sunshine.

Chapter Seven

Blue Moon Clover

The Black Stag was very wary of them as they approached. Few visitors ever found their way into the Forgotten Meadow. The fairies, fox, and squirrel thought that the Black Stag was a little intimidating, with his immense size and foreboding expression, so they approached him slowly. Firefly and the black squirrel explained the reason for their visit and appealed to the stag to help them find blue moon clover.

He stared at them with large, glittering black eyes for a minute before he spoke. Then he told them, "I knew it must be important; I seldom have visitors. Only the dwarf knows were to find me. And no creature ever strays into the Forgotten Meadow. The only way this meadow can be found is by seeking it. And it is only sought if the dwarf sends someone looking for me.

"Yes, I will find blue moon clover for you. It is very fortunate that you came this week. I can only find blue moon clover with my antlers, and I will be shedding them next week. I shed them each spring. Then they are regrown over the summer. I cannot find blue moon clover during the summertime." Then the Black Stag added, "It will be best if you ride on my antlers. When the clover is revealed, you can jump off and pick it. And you should pick the entire clover, including the stem. The whole plant has healing properties."

The fox left the group and bounded away into the forest, as the black squirrel told them, "He's going to send a message to the brownies. They will be transporting the blue moon clover back to the black squirrel colonies."

The fairies very excitedly flew up and landed on the stag's enormous antlers. They were smooth and a bit slippery, so the fairies had to hold on tightly. Madam June Beetle gave each fairy three bags to hold the picked clover.

The fairies sat in the forks of the stag's antlers. The black squirrel stayed in the middle of the meadow and curled into a little ball for a rest while the fairies did their work. Then the stag lowered his head. Walking in slow circles, outward from the center of the meadow, he swept his antlers back and forth across the ground. "Do you see it?" he asked.

Looking closely, the fairies did indeed see blue moon clover. As the antlers passed over the thick clumps of dark green clover, tiny patches of brilliant blue were revealed, glowing and shimmering softly.

"Pick it quickly," the stag instructed, "before the blue glow fades."

Thistle and Marigold jumped off first and began picking the stems of bright blue clover. Then Madam Monarch and Firefly flew down. As Thistle and Marigold flew back up to their perches on the antlers, Periwinkle and Madam June Beetle alighted and flew down. Working in pairs, they filled all of the sacks they had brought and knotted the ends so the clover would stay securely in the bags.

They had covered nearly half the meadow when the stag said, "That should be plenty. I have a pretty good knowledge of black squirrel numbers. You have picked enough for every black squirrel, and then some."

As the fairies finished closing the sacks, a bald eagle and a peregrine falcon swooped low over the meadow. The birds landed, and two brownies slid from their backs. The fairies were overjoyed to see Brownie Christopher and Brownie Alan.

The Black Stag told the fairies, "This is amazing: I have had more visitors in one day than have ever found their way into the Forgotten Meadow before."

The brownies knew exactly what needed to be done, and knew that time was very important. They quickly loaded the sacks of blue moon clover onto the eagle and falcon. The boys did not stop to talk to the fairies, but mounted the birds right away, eager to set off at once. But Alan did manage to wink at Marigold before the birds took flight.

The Black Stag called after them. "One clover per squirrel will be enough. It is very powerful."

Chapter Eight

The Shadow of Death
and the Light of Life

arrying a single stem of blue moon clover, Firefly flew to the black squirrel. He was very weak. She took his head gently in her hands, trying to get him to eat the clover. He raised his head slightly, but only to whisper. "It's too late."

"No!" said Firefly fearfully. "It's not too late, eat it," she urged. The other fairies and the Black Stag looked on sadly.

But Firefly was determined. She was glowing more brightly than ever before and laid a small hand on the squirrel's chest. Light flowed from her hand and covered the squirrel, and

he seemed to gain a small measure of strength. He raised his head again and tried to eat the clover. However, before he could eat it, the fairies noticed a black shadow creeping up to where the squirrel lay.

The Black Stag said softly, "It is the Shadow of Death. He has come for the squirrel."

"No," said Firefly quietly, but firmly. Then louder, she repeated, "No! It is not his time."

Keeping one hand on the black squirrel's chest, she reached out with the other hand and touched the shadow. Firefly winced with pain as she did this, but the shadow retreated a few inches. Her light continued to cover the squirrel, protecting him. Then, unexpectedly, Firefly's entire body ignited with a brilliant flash of gold and orange light. The other fairies shielded their eyes from the blinding brightness and backed away.

When the light subsided, the Shadow of Death had disappeared. The black squirrel was sitting up, eating the clover; and Firefly was sitting on the ground about a foot away from him, breathing hard, as though she had run very fast.

She shook her head in amazement and said, "I never knew." She took a moment to catch her breath before explaining further. "The light that leads me—it is life. It is so small, only about the size of a grain of sand inside me. I thought it was just a guiding light, but it is much more. It is life."

Madam June Beetle helped her up and put an arm around the young fairy's shoulders, hugging her. Firefly looked from face to face at each of her friends. With an expression of wonder and surprise, she said in awe, "It is very powerful."

The black squirrel looked better almost immediately, and he was anxious to be getting home to his colony. The gray fox had returned to the meadow and would be traveling with the squirrel, to help him until he regained full strength.

Each of the fairies hugged the black squirrel and wished him a safe journey home. Firefly hugged him last, and the squirrel whispered in her ear, "Thank you for saving my life. I will never forget you." Firefly gave him a smile and an extra hug.

The squirrel also said goodbye to the Black Stag, thanking him; then he bounded away towards home, the fox trotting beside him.

The fairies bid farewell to the Black Stag and thanked him earnestly for his help. Then the group traveled back through the white meadow and the purple meadow. They decided to camp for the night on the edge of the forest next to the purple meadow. The Forgotten Forest was very beautiful, with the trees all budding spring leaves, and wildflowers beginning to bloom every color imaginable.

While they ate a satisfying dinner of peanut butter and marshmallow créme sandwiches, raspberries, and lemon jellybeans, the fairies debated whether or not they wanted to stop back by the dwarf's home. The group decided that although they would have liked to have seen him again, and Firecracker, they did not particularly want to know if the squit was real or imagined.

"Mysteries are fun," said Firefly. "Some things should be left unknown."

As they admired the sunset, breathed the evening breeze, and watched the new springtime life bursting out everywhere, Periwinkle discovered a small pile of ghost leaves that had come to rest for winter under a hollowed log. The heart-shaped leaves were a pale gold color, almost white; and they were see-through because only the veins of the leaves remained, like a leaf skeleton.

Periwinkle explained that the ghost leaves were created when insects ate the leaf, but left the tougher veins. "Some leaves are so full of life," she told them, "that even when they die, they cannot completely disappear."

Each of the fairies took one ghost leaf home with her as a souvenir of their journey. They left the others for the forest to keep, or for someone else to find.

A week after returning home, Firefly received a nut message from the black squirrel. He thanked her again for her help, and let her know that the black squirrels were all cured and healthy. Included with the note was a tiny golden acorn, just like the one the black squirrel had given to the dwarf.

Though she was very pleased with the gift, Firefly was much more thankful for

the news that the squirrels were alive and
well. Life was far more valuable and important than any golden treasure.

The End

Fairy Fun

The Nameless Squit

A dwarf recently moved into an abandoned silver mine and discovered that a squit was already living there. They were overjoyed to see one another and quickly adopted each other. Squits are often given names relating to their colors. However, the dwarf had never seen a squit of such a pale green color and was stumped when trying to give his new pet a name. (He didn't think Minty or Pistachio quite fit.)

As far as we know, the dwarf is still struggling with this problem. There is a magical way that we might be able to help. Because dwarves use powerful mind magic, they often send their thoughts on journeys around the world to pick up messages. They most often communicate with others through books and the number twelve. To help the dwarf, please think up a name. Then write your suggestion on a piece of paper or stationery. Be sure to draw a picture of the squit next to his name. Fold the paper into the shape of a bookmark, and place it in your favorite book exactly at page twelve. Dwarf thoughts take two full days to circle the earth, so make sure the bookmark stays on page twelve during that time. Keep the bookmark over the years because the squit may eventually want to visit the person who helped to name him, and the lure of the bookmark might be the only way he can find you.

FAIRY FACTS

Chameleon Lizards

Chameleons are very unique among lizards. In addition to their ability to change colors, they have pincer-like feet to allow them to climb trees easily. Chameleons also have very long tongues, sometimes even longer than their bodies, which they use to snatch insects. They also have eyes that can move independently from one another, so the chameleons can keep constant watch on their surroundings.

Blue Moons

As the fairies learn from their Fairy Handbooks, a blue moon can be either a second full moon in a single month or a third full moon in any season that has four full moons. Both are called "blue moons" and while both are rare, over the next twenty years there are going to be seventeen blue moons! There will be no blue moons during the years 2011, 2014 and 2017. The last blue moon to occur was on May 31st 2007. Where were you that day? Did you know it was going to be a blue moon? Did you see it? If not, don't worry, it is not the most special blue moon ever to shine because every nineteen years, there are two blue moons in the same year! The last time this happened it was in 1999 when there was a blue moon in January and again in March. Can you figure out when the next year there will be two blue moons is?

If you want to catch all of the blue moons (of both kinds) through 2010, here is a handy list:

May 2008

Third full moon in a season of four full moons

Dec. 2009

Second full moon in month

Nov. 2010

Third full moon in a season of four full moons

Enjoy the moon watching!

Inside you is the power to do anything

The Fairy Chronicles

. . . the adventures continue

Marigold and the Feather of Hope

"Inside you is the power to do anything"

The Fairy Chronicles

Marigold and the Feather of Hope,
the Journey Begins

J. H. SWEET

Like most nine year old girls, Beth wants to spend her summer goofing off. Unfortunately her parents are making her spend two whole weeks with her crazy Aunt Evelyn. This time however, Aunt Evelyn has a secret to tell...

Somewhat alarmed, Beth slid sideways in her seat putting about a foot of extra distance between her and her aunt. Aunt Evelyn was leaning forward, obviously very excited about something. Her dark brown eyes, now flashing with flecks of orange and black, were a bit scary. Beth had never seen these colors in her aunt's eyes before. They both took a deep breath, staring at each other as the room became very still.

Beth felt a tingling sensation, as though something very important was about to happen. Aunt Evelyn continued to stare at her. Just as Beth was thinking of having another sip of soda, her aunt stated calmly, "You are a marigold fairy."

Discovering her new powers, making new and magical friends and being sent on a super important mission make for one really exciting summer. But if Beth, now known as Marigold, doesn't find the Feather of Hope it might be the last good summer anyone ever has.

Now Available in Bookstores and Online

Dragonfly and the Web of Dreams

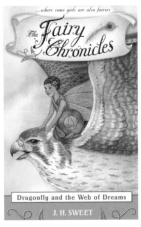

...where some girls are also fairies

The Fairy Chronicles

Dragonfly and the Web of Dreams

J. H. SWEET

Dragonfly and her closest friends, Marigold, Thistle, and Firefly have all been having terrible nightmares all week long. So it comes as no surprise that the problem is getting worse, and not just for fairies. An emergency Fairy Circle is called...

"Welcome, welcome! Attention, attention everyone! We are here to discuss the problem of the nightmares. First of all, we need to thank the doves."

Madam Toad gestured to one side of the gathering where several tired and bedraggled looking doves were cooing sleepily. "They have been working overtime, delivering good dreams to help balance out the dream problem. It would be much worse if not for their efforts."

There was polite applause and Madam Toad continued. "The Web of Dreams has been destroyed. I went with the Sandman yesterday to confirm this. It is not clear who destroyed it or how anyone knew its location. But it must be rebuilt quickly or the problem will worsen."

The fairy team must find the Dream Spider, discover the cause of the Web's destruction, and get a new one built before the whole world succumbs to nightmares and good dreams become a thing of the past.

Now Available in Bookstores and Online

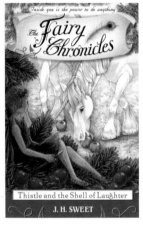

The Shell of Laughter has been stolen from Staid, the Elf! Madam Toad sends Thistle and her friends to recapture the Shell before all laughter is gone forever. But a very dangerous enemy has control of the Shell.

Killjoy Crosspatch, the Spirit of Sorrow, stared at them without speaking. Thistle, Marigold, and Dragonfly thought he was the most disgusting and foul creature they had ever seen. "Where is the shell?" demanded Staid.

Killjoy Crosspatch didn't speak. Instead, a wide, uneven smile crept across his ugly face, and he slowly raised his hands in front of him. From his dripping palms, a dark gray, smoky cloud began to seep. It slowly crept towards the elf, the hedgehog, the leprechaun, Madam Robin, and the fairies.

They tried to take cover behind several of the rocks, but the oozing darkness followed them. It seemed there was no escape from the cloud of sorrow.

Can they do it? Will the fairies defeat the Spirit of Sorrow and return the Shell to its rightful owner? More important, will the world ever get to laugh again?

Now Available in Bookstores and Online

Spiderwort and the Princess of Haiku

The Princess of Haiku has been kidnapped and if she is not found and saved, the whole world will forget the simple pleasures in life!

Would anyone want to live without knowing the pleasure of a poem or the sweet smell of roses? The fairies hope we will never have to find out!

Unfortunately, the only thing they have to go on is a confusing riddle from a particularly unhelpful oak tree. Luckily, for us all, Spiderwort is one of the smartest fairies anywhere and if anyone can solve the puzzles and save the Princess it is this amazing fairy team!

Available in Bookstores and Online in September 2007

118

Periwinkle and the Cave of Courage

Once every hundred years, the courage of humanity begins to fail. It takes a coordinated effort from the entire magic community to restore the Cave of Courage so that we can all bravely face the challenges in our lives.

This century, Mother Nature has chosen a dwarf, a leprechaun, a gnome, a troll, two brownies, and four fairies to participate. With four fairies involved usually no challenge would be too difficult, but now they must rely on the help of others, something that not everyone is good at...

Available in Bookstores and Online in September 2007

About the Author

J. H. Sweet has always looked for the magic in the everyday. She has an imaginary dog named Jellybean Ebenezer Beast. Her hobbies include hiking, photography, knitting, and basketry. She also enjoys watching a variety of movies and sports. Her favorite superhero is her husband, with Silver Surfer coming in a close second. She loves many of the same things the fairies love, including live oak trees, mockingbirds, weathered terra-cotta, butterflies, bees, and cypress knees. In the fairy game of "If I were a jellybean, what flavor would I be?" she would be green apple. J. H. Sweet lives with her husband in South Texas and has a degree in English from Texas State University.

About the Illustrator

Ever since she was a little girl, Tara Larsen Chang has been captivated by intricate illustrations in fairy tales and children's books. Since earning her BFA in Illustration from Brigham Young University, her illustrations have appeared in numerous children's books and magazines. When she is not drawing and painting in her studio, she can be found working in her gardens to make sure that there are plenty of havens for visiting fairies.